The Frog Band
and the Mystery of
Lion Castle

JIM SMITH

First published in Great Britain by World's Work Ltd, 1978
Fircone Books edition 2011
Text and illustrations copyright © Jim Smith 1978
ISBN 978-1-907700-02-6

Visit our website at www.firconebooks.com
Design by Dot Little. Printed and bound in China.

FSC
www.fsc.org

MIX
Paper from
responsible sources
FSC® C008047

Fircone Books

"Heave, one, two, three ..." chanted the Frog Band as they pushed their broken-down lorry over the drawbridge of Lion Castle one New Year's Eve, scattering mud and leaves everywhere. "Oh, no!" gasped Mrs MacOtter. "I've just this minute cleaned there!"

Johann S. Frog raised his hat politely and said, "Excuse me, Ma'am, we are the famous Frog Band and, as you can see, we are looking for help."

The clatter on the drawbridge attracted the elderly owner of the castle, who leisurely emerged from a doorway. "Hello chaps. Having a spot of bother? Brooker Lion at your service!" Johann introduced himself and his Band, and asked if they might borrow a tool kit. Brooker was only too delighted to help and, as Godfrey disappeared under the lorry, he invited the other frogs to see inside the castle.

First he took them to his laboratory, which was his pride and joy.
Johann was very impressed by a strange cabinet with many knobs and
switches. "That is my wireless set," announced Brooker proudly. "I can
receive messages from all over the world!" All the frogs were greatly
mystified by the crackling sounds from it.

Meanwhile, high above the castle, another frog was also mystified. Alphonse le Flic, eminent detective, was in his gas balloon, and he was lost. He was on his way to an International Conference of Sleuths, but he had been blown off course. He was already late, but now he feared he would have to miss it altogether. Leaning over the edge of his basket, he emptied some sand ballast.

Suddenly, he was thrown into a corner of the basket and showered with maps, compasses and cameras as the basket swung crazily beneath the balloon. The air was filled with a loud tearing sound and a violent hissing! Staggering to his feet, Alphonse realised that the balloon had been caught by a high, wire aerial mast on one of the turrets of the castle below.

Slowly the balloon sank to the ground as the gas escaped through the large hole. Alphonse looked for his repair kit, but it was too late. "Catch this rope and guide me down!" he yelled to the group of frogs who were standing gaping in the castle courtyard.

Safely on the ground, Alphonse greeted his old friends the Frog Band with delight, and explained his problem to their host. "No trouble my boy," said Brooker sympathetically, "I can soon make you some more gas. But not tonight, it's getting late!"

That night, as they sat round the log fire in the Great Hall, Brooker Lion told his guests of his ancestor, Clarence de Lyon, who had disappeared from his study on New Year's Eve many years ago, when the castle had been under siege from his enemies.

Ever since then, it was said that his ghost walked the castle every New Year's Eve, and no villager would go near the castle at that time.

The next morning dawned bright and *very* cold. The surrounding countryside was white with frost, and the moat was covered with a solid sheet of ice, inches thick.

While Godfrey Frog donned his overalls and started work on the lorry's engine once again, Brooker Lion set up his equipment to produce the gas for Alphonse's balloon.

Finding himself with nothing to do, Shortie Frog wandered off on his own to explore the castle's dungeon. To his disappointment, he found it had been used as a storeroom and was now full of unwanted bits and pieces piled up over the years. "Never mind," Shortie said to himself. "Perhaps I'll find something of old Clarence de Lyon," and he began to sift through the junk.

Right at the back of the old dungeon, Shortie came across a rusty lever set in the stone wall. Curiosity overcame him and, although he knew he shouldn't meddle, he pulled it down.

Immediately, the underground room echoed with a fearsome grinding noise, which ended in a long, loud gurgle! Shortie was terrified! He dived beneath an old sofa, and pulled a dust-sheet over his ears.

In the meantime, up in the courtyard, the balloon had been re-filled and was straining at its tethering ropes. Alphonse was delighted with the results, and offered to take Brooker up for a ride in the balloon, before he set off for his Conference.

Warmly wrapped up in an enormous overcoat, Brooker Lion heaved himself into the basket.

Godfrey Frog, who had finished tinkering with the lorry, had come across an old gun in a corner, and now he dragged it onto the drawbridge in order to fire a salute as the balloon ascended. Philip the cornet player caught the festive mood and climbed the battlements, ready to blow a fanfare.

As Alphonse and Brooker slowly rose out of the courtyard, Godfrey Frog put a match to the gun fuse and, up above, Philip lifted the cornet to his lips.

With a sickening thud, the grapnel caught Philip from behind, and he dropped his cornet right down into the upturned muzzle of Godfrey's gun!

There was a red flash and a huge cloud of smoke as the cornet was shot clean through the balloon!

CRASH! The basket plummeted downwards, smashed through the thick ice, and disappeared from view! "Save them, they'll be drowned!" cried Johann, trying to make himself heard above the clamour and confusion of the courtyard.

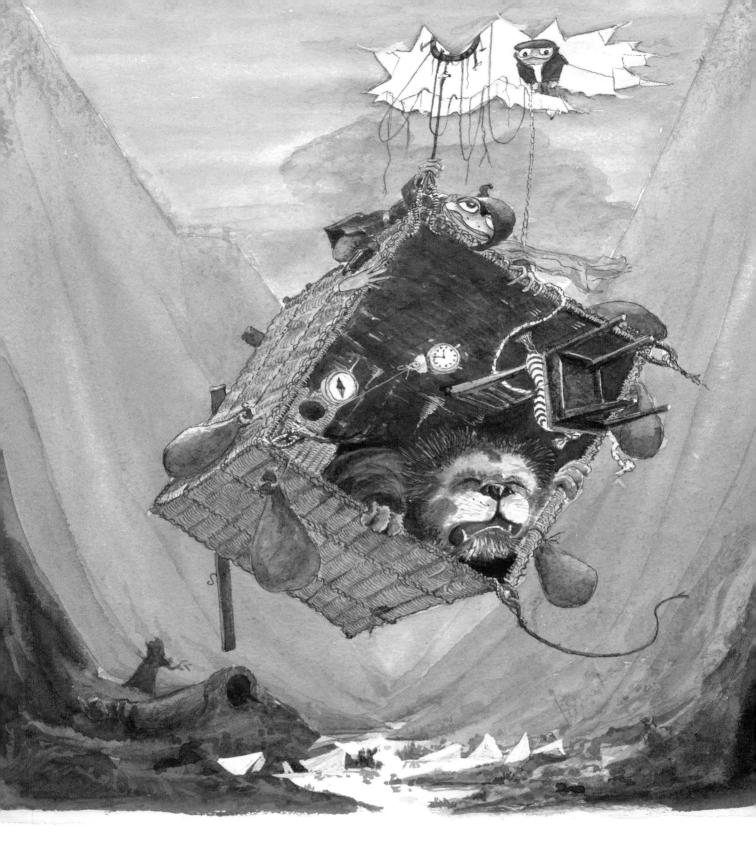

However, underneath the ice, Brooker Lion and Alphonse le Flic were still in the basket, swinging wildly. The moat was waterless! Unknown to everyone, Shortie Frog's mysterious grinding lever had emptied the moat!

"Don't panic!" ordered Alphonse, as he produced his magnifying glass and a torch. "I'm going to investigate the situation." He climbed out of the basket on to the slimy floor of the moat. Creeping forward, he peered into the gloom. "It's all clear!" he called back to Brooker, "you can come down."

Down in the dungeon, Shortie Frog had been amusing himself with an old phonograph he had found behind the sofa. With only one cylinder to play, he soon became bored and thought he should go back to the others. Halfway upstairs, he worried about the lever, which was still in the wrong position. "I had better put it back to where it was," he muttered reluctantly. As soon as he did so, he heard a distant rumbling sound that was getting closer every minute!

Alphonse was bravely peering in every shadow, when he too heard the rumble. Nearer it came, and louder and louder! "The water!" he yelled, "It's coming back. RUN!" and the two ran as fast as they could to find some way out of the moat before the oncoming rush of water.

Just as Alphonse was beginning to think this was the end of his promising career, he spied a doorway. Gasping for breath, he pulled Brooker through.

The steep stairs behind the door led Alphonse and Brooker up and up until they came to a blank wall! "There must be a secret panel!" breathed Alphonse, as he frantically tapped the wall to find the spring that would release the hidden door. "Oh hurry!" panicked the old lion.

Unaffected by all the excitement, Mrs MacOtter was cleaning the study. She was interrupted by a scratching noise coming from behind the wall. "The ghost!" she thought in horror, and quickly reassured herself, "but surely not in daylight!" Then she froze as the portrait of Clarence de Lyon slowly creaked open and two very muddy creatures tumbled out onto her polished floor.

Brooker looked puzzled for a while, and then he shouted, "Well done Alphonse! You've solved the mystery of Lion Castle! Don't you see my boy?" He carried on. "The castle can't be haunted after all! Old Clarence didn't vanish into thin air all those years ago, he used the passage and escaped across the moat."

The following summer, the Frog Band held a series of concerts in the courtyard, and Alphonse returned to give joy-rides in his balloon. As Brooker Lion greeted yet another of the tourists who flocked to the castle now the rumour of the ghost had been lifted, he jingled his money pocket and blessed the day when chance had led Alphonse le Flic, eminent detective, and the famous Frog Band to Lion Castle.